STARSEED

Starseed

Stephen Guy

Cover Art and Design by

Aaron Bilawchuk

Interior Art by Rebecca Piazza

THE SEVENTH TERRACE

CANADA

For Sarah and Rob, for their hard work and their creative vision.

Humanity looked in awe upon the beauty and the everlasting duration of creation. The exquisite sky flooded with sunlight. The majesty of the dark night lit by celestial torches as the holy planetary powers trace their paths in the heavens in fixed and steady metre – ordering the growth of things with their secret infusions.

— Hermes Trismegistus, Corpus Hermeticum

Immortal Amaranth,

that once in Eden bloomed

fast by the tree of life,

but soon, for man's offence,

to Heaven removed,

where first it grew

and there still grows

its flower high,

where it shades the font of life.

- John Milton, Paradise Lost

I: PRINCIPAL

Don't ever touch the principal. Out of all my Father's advice, this alone I took.

My parents had vested upon me a trust born of my grandfather's great wealth and at the age of twenty-one I was free to do as I pleased. My father was always mindful of that old adage, "the first generation builds, the second consolidates, the third squanders." He would not see me a squanderer. In this alone I made him proud, for never have I touched the principal. In the rest of my course, in my entertainments and distractions, in my worldly learning pursued at the expense of academic education, and in my particular tastes and peculiar acquisitions, his puritan soul saw nothing noble. However, the principal secure, he restrained himself from mentioning it. There was peace in my mother's house, at least on those rare occasions when I attended my childhood home. I might do as I please and not as I ought, but the family fortune is secure and the better part of the family name thereby.

As for the rest, it is neither an empty boast nor a begging confession to say this much: I have eaten the fruit right off of the tree.

II: RITUAL

Although I had given up my formal academic pursuits when liberated by family money, I had stayed in contact with my old Professor. Doctor Cornelius was a medical man by degree but a botanist by inclination. He never failed to welcome me into his house. Here he maintained a quiet and studious retirement, devoted to the collection of rare scientific manuscripts, and a large laboratory and greenhouse wherein he attempted all manner of hybridization. He had but one servant, an enormous, glowering Bashi-Bazouk who seemed both mute and nameless. I had but to send word to the Professor that I was in town and within hours the Bashi-Bazouk would be at my door, black-bearded and silent, with a card upon which was written a formal invitation to dinner with the Professor. The brute would wait while I dressed, and then, with an alacrity that belied his imposing bulk he'd take me by carriage to the residence of my old friend.

The Professor greeted me at the door, formally, and led me to the dining room. The meal was a mostly silent affair served by the giant, and, done with our repast we'd proceed to an atrium behind the house, there to smoke and partake of some brandy. The Professor was not without connections of his own and his brandy was always excellent. We talked of many things over an 1877 Martell. He spoke of his botanical hybrids in passionate detail, and I of my travels, although I omitted anything other than the architecture and botany of the places I had been out of a sense of decorum towards the old man. I had on this occasion managed to bring him a gift, something for his library. Prior to commencing our third brandy I produced the book and described it so:

"Herr Professor, here, for you, a gift. It is a Pharmacopeia of uncertain provenance, untitled. It is hand-written and illuminated, certainly preceding any incunabula I obtained for you previously. Two-hundred and seventy-two pages of vellum organized into eighteen quires. The binding and cover bear the seal of the Collego Romano and is certainly not original. It is, unfortunately, encrypted. No key to the cipher has yet to reveal itself. A separate letter left inside dates from 1666, written by one John March – almost certainly an alias – seeking help from an unidentified party in deciphering the alphabet within. I thought that if not exactly useful, you might at least find it entertaining. As a botanist you may not need the alphabet to decipher the illustrations. A great many are of plants and flowers, and even seeds. Climbing vines and fruit too. The seller believed the manuscript to have belonged to the Sicilian King Rudolfo, a scholar of some note in his own right, although as I said, provenance is obscure."

Doctor Cornelius took the book carefully. He ruffled the pages with his thumb and listened to them. He then ruffled the pages a second time, smelling them. He set the book down then and spoke to me.

"You have made an old man very happy," he said, with a softness in his eyes. This was thanks enough, and we returned to our brandies.

The evening was done after a fourth brandy, after which even I, who had some experience with brandy to put it modestly, was feeling a little slow of both limb and wit.

The Professor walked me to the door. The Bazouk was waiting with the carriage. The Professor shook my hand with both of his, and then spoke clearly and with great intensity, the effects of the brandy aside. "You were the finest of my students. It is a shame you left. But I understand. Tomorrow night, an hour after dinner, I am performing a great experiment, a fantastical hybridization. I dared not to speak of it earlier but the book – ah, the book. You found it, you bought it, you gave it to me. You will understand. You will not judge me. I cannot send my man. I need his strength with me in the laboratory. But, if you hire a carriage or some other means and can meet me in here in my lab at the appointed hour, you will witness something marvelous."

He held my right hand in his own a long time, and with his left gripped hard upon my wrist. I hesitated. I was unnerved a little by his fierce hold, but finally nodded my assent. After all, he was my Professor, my mentor, and more importantly my friend. There was nothing he could ask for that I would decline.

III: EXPERIMENT

I hired livery the next night and made my way to the Professor's. The hired driver had not the deft touch of the Professor's man, and we did not make good time. I arrived late. I paid the man and furthermore dismissed him from having to return me to my suite. I'd find another way, or perhaps lodge with the Professor. The city is one thing by day and quite another at night. A man who lives as I do, with the means at my disposal, was probably safer with the Bazouk than a hired driver, and a barely competent one at that.

No one answered my knock. Feeling more than a little ashamed at my lateness, and constructing my apology in my head, I walked in unattended and made my way to the laboratory.

The Professor's house was old, and although well within the city's growth it had once been a small manor with an orchard and various functional buildings and appurtenances of sorts on the grounds. All that was left of these was the orchard, marvelously husbanded by my friend, and the laboratory, a building that he had converted to his uses from what had once been a fine carriage house. In between there was a small lawn. With the orchard trees and the carriage house bordering it, it seemed more like the atrium of some ancient Roman senator's Apennine villa than an open space. I crossed it, inhaling the wonderful fragrances of the orchard and the night, and entered the laboratory.

Inside the laboratory were a thousand objects, too many to take in at once and cataloguing them would be an exercise in both mnemonics and science that I do not possess. It was primarily a greenhouse, and if there were a thousand objects inside, there were a thousand more plants. The Professor had removed/renovated the southern exposure to be a wall of windows so that during the day there would be plenty of light for his innumerable specimens. At night one could look up and see the stars should all interior light be extinguished.

He had been in the habit of using old crates and shipping pallets to rest his collection upon, and many of these crates also contained soil or fertilizer and even the manures of exotic kine and fowl or even, as he told me once, bats. Some flowers bloomed by day and some yet by night, and the place was an explosion of color. Fruits, some of which I had never seen before, hung heavily from sagging boughs or in pregnant clusters.

I doubted that the world had seen some of them. Tendrils and creepers and vines walked and climbed across the floors and walls even unto the roof. It was an instant concern of mine that they conspired to pull the place down, and I mentioned this to the Professor. The Professor dissented of course, telling me that he thought it more probable that they were instead holding the place up.

There were all manner of sacks and bags, filled with seeds and pods, leaves and mulches. The sounds of bees drifted down as they moved in accordance with their endless labors. There was light – a goodly amount of light – by multiple oil lamps, and by this I saw that he had drawn to the center of this great space a curious grouping. There was a large pool of sorts, made from the cut-off end of the most massive cask or barrel I had ever seen. It was fully ten feet in diameter, its iron-bound planks three feet high and filled almost to the brim with dark, stagnant water. On this stillness floated some large examples of what I deemed to be lotus of some sort, for upon first impression I could think only of lotus as living in such an arrangement. They were heavy-petaled and cotton-white, and drifted slowly and aimlessly across the calm of their artificial harbor.

On either side of the lotus-pool were surgical tables, heavy oaken things, tilted to a forty-five-degree angle. Strapped onto each table was a young woman covered for modesty in a white sheet. Their necks and shoulders were bare. Neither looked at me as I came in. Each stared at the ceiling far above, as if lost in some personal reverie. I had seen the look before, in many places on my travels, and I assumed they had been given some soporific, perhaps laudanum, as it was commonly available and not at all unpleasant.

"Ah!" The Professor said, spying me. "The wayward apprentice arrives at last."

I tried to demure, and wondered at "apprentice", but he ignored me. "Come," he said, and motioned that I could help he and the Bazouk dress, for there were rubber aprons and rubber gloves, long bracers that reach to each man's elbows and even slightly above, and it took one man helping the other to be properly fitted. While I fitted the two men the Professor summarized the philosophy of what he was about to attempt as such:

"In 1898 a colleague managed an expedition to Antarctica. There he disappeared, as did every member of the adventure, right down to the last Patagonian porter and the ship's captain, a Finn as hard as a coffin nail. The Finn was well beloved of the Tsar of Russia, who had been his master for twenty years, and was a man who could be trusted in all manner of adverse circumstances. At any rate, botany not being central to my friend's exploration he had been in the habit of sending me samples and even seed, and so I came to this: the Star Flower."

At this he gestured at the strange lotus-like plants, which seemed to idle upon the water in their pool languidly, as if trying to be still rather than being merely inert. The Professor continued:

"Of all of the samples he sent, the seeds of these," and again he gestured at the lotus-thing, "Were the most unique, the most interesting, and the most captivating. He had said only that he had traded some distilled spirits – a middling cognac if I recall his letter correctly – for them to an elderly Jesuit, an otherwise erudite man turned mad by his time in the rain forests of the Amazon in his missionary past, and the distilled spirits that were his declining present. This Jesuit made the preposterous claim that the seeds were from a place other than our earth, and possibly even our solar system. 'Beyond the stars,' my colleague told me. 'Beyond the stars.' He insisted upon this and would hear no other thesis.

"Right or wrong – imagine for one moment if you will of what strange light birthed them, and of what unknown sun brought them to flower? That may seem like nonsense to you but remember: the ancient sage Anaxagoras used the term Panspermia to describe one theory of the origin of life here on earth as early as the 5th century BC. Panspermia is the theory that microorganisms or biochemical compounds from outer space are responsible for bringing life to Earth. If it is mad it is madness friended with the company of great minds. Anaxagoras, Berzelius, Richter, Kelvin and even our contemporary Arrhenius have hypothesized the same."

As he spoke I watched the flowers, their thin mauve tendrils spreading beneath them like veins, their obscene and alluring white petals folded against one another in uneven lines, and it seemed to me that they drifted – no, moved – to the sound of the Professor's voice, coming closer to the edge of the pool beside which we prepared he and the Bazouk in their laboratory garments.

"Once I determined the calculus of the heat, the humidity, and environment – all of which you see before you now," he said, gesturing at the painstakingly assembled laboratory, "I was able to raise the seedlings to the beautiful creatures you see before you."

At this I stopped. He had used the word "creatures" with a subtle emphasis. He was not the type of man to make something from nothing, or to be careless in his terminology or his applications thereby.

"But my beautiful creatures, my star-children, I could not make reproduce. How they procreate, how they pollinate, how they spread, these things remained a mystery to me. Light I gave them, according the proportion they desired, and darkness in an exact amount. I gave them still water too, black and unmoving, all of it. But still, no Star Flowers."

With that he leaned into the water and picked up one of the flowers, whose white petals stretched visibly towards him, stretched and expanded, reaching, reaching for his hands as might a friend, as might a lover. I remained silent. The Professor's words echoed in my ears and the vision of the Star Flower reaching up to him had rendered me mute. The Professor then nodded to the Bazouk, who carefully picked up the second Star Flower and they lifted the pair out of the umbral pool and held them up at arm's length, trailing water from their lolling tendrils. Without a word they placed the flowers on the faces of the sheeted women strapped to the leather surgical tables.

The folds on the flowers began to swell, and the tendrils flowed with a dark hematic as they latched on to the women. They seemed to both invade and caress, to take possession and to soothe at the same time. The girl on the right of the two tables, who had very long hair of a red-gold color, began to struggle mightily, and as the sheet fell away from her I could see where she had been belted on to the table at the ankles, just above the knees, the waist and the shoulder too – and that the position of the last two belts denied her the use of her hands. She shook her head from side to side and cried out wildly until the swelling folds of the Star Flower stifled her. Even then, her hands remained balled up into fists.

The second girl, her dark hair unbound just like the first's, did not struggle or attempt to evade the Star Flower's folds and tendrils at all. Rather, she rose to it. She arched her back and lifted up her head, exposing her throat. There was a blush on her that spoke of the heat of her body. I could see the purple of the Star Flower's tendrils working their way underneath the surface of her skin at the throat. She arched her back and thrust her hips up from the table and held them high, and had she not been lying down I would describe her as ascending, her weight on the balls of her naked feet, while she stretched to touch the sky. I knew, without a doubt, my instinct honed by years of the dedicated practice of innumerable debaucheries, that she was in the throes of a lasting and recurring passion.

I thrilled to this.

The Star Flowers, deep into the two subjects now, their enveloping petals lush and tumescent, began to hum via the gentle and rapid vibrations of those self-same folds. The effect, although alien, was of some lullaby of triumph, some song of the night to ease the frightened through to a glorious dawn. Each girl held her position through the whole of this whispered and sibilant song. The dark-haired Venus, open-mouthed underneath the flower, touched the angled bed only at naked heel and shoulder, and arched her way into her fiery flight. I saw her hands, open-palmed, with fingers outspread. I heard the sharp intake of her breath, then the "ahh" of controlled exhalation. The fairer girl, eyes tightly shut and fists held so tightly closed as to make her fingers alabaster, remained as rigid on the white sheets as a specimen in an anatomist's laboratory and did not make a sound.

After a brief interval the Star Flowers ceased to hum, then retracted their purplish tendrils from under the skin of their hosts. At this the Professor and his Bazouk moved quickly to the girls to remove the Star Flowers from the girl's faces and replace them in the artificial grotto made from that singularly large barrel. Each of the flowers came away from their girl's face with the soft sound of something sticky and sweet being pulled apart and emitted a smell both floral and musky – animal even – but pleasant too. The Professor and the Bazouk very carefully placed the Star Flowers in the dark water.

I moved quickly to the dark-haired woman. During the removal of the plant the sheet that had covered her had come off entirely leaving her exposed to the room, and although it was warmer than the night outside I still felt she should not suffer any discomfort of exposure, even in light of what I had just seen. I picked up the sheet but lingered a bit before covering her, seeing that she had, by some depilatory art, removed all of her pubic hair. Her vulva was slightly darker than the rest of her complexion, flushed with passion I was sure, and her own folds and creases at the center of her sex were darker yet and glistened like joy. When at last I covered her with the sheet and drew it up to her shoulders she opened her eyes and smiled beatifically.

"Are you alright?" I asked.

She laughed, and sat up, wrapping herself in the sheet.

The Professor and the Bazouk were working to restore the fairer girl to consciousness. Their ministrations were at first orderly, and then frantic, and then ceased altogether, each man at the same time, and without a word. The girl was dead. The sheet she was wrapped in was soaked. She had, in her terror, urinated before passing away in the embrace of the Star Flower. The Professor stripped his rubber gloves off in anger and threw them to the floor, then rubbed his temples. The Bazouk stepped back and looked at the Professor, awaiting instructions either verbal or tacit.

It was the dark-haired girl, braiding her hair into a single, long queue while the Professor and Bazouk labored to save the dead girl, who spoke first. "Jenny," she said, with a trace of some eastern European accent. "Her name was Jenny. Irish Jenny or

Dublin Jenny or just plain Jenny. Whichever the gentlemen who had the means to obtain her company preferred."

IV: CONFESSION

The Professor walked over to the waters hosting the Star Flowers, now drifting aimlessly. One would have thought them nothing but water plants, pretty enough and of unusual size and structure, but not creatures that sang, things of flowing blood and passionate flesh filled with an animating spirit that made love and caressed.

Without looking back at us he said, "Pay Imbroglio whatever he asks, and set Jenny gently into the sea."

The big Bazouk understood immediately and without answering the Professor he gestured at me, and we rolled Irish Jenny up into the sheet in which she had so recently lain alive, and then moved her into a canvas bag the like of which sailors transport their gear in. We carried the poor, slight girl out to the carriage and lay her in the back. The Bazouk took a trio of paving stones piled up from some recent repair to the Professor's driveway and set them beside her, along with a few lengths of rope.

The Bazouk readied the horses and I helped the dark-haired woman, now braided and dressed, onto the seat and sat beside her. In due course the Bazouk set upon the cart, his great weight tilting it his way enough that the girl had to grab onto my arm in order not to slide into the Bazouk. Quietly, then, with no "haw" or "gee" or shouted commands the Bazouk drove the carriage out into the darkness. The girl kept her arm in mine the whole time. No one spoke.

In due course we came to a quiet dock. There were none but us there, and not even gas lamps to light the way. The stars of the Pleiades, and indeed a thousand or hundred thousand others were plainly visible in the firmament above. I gently detached myself from my ward's arm and stepped off the carriage with the Bazouk and went to the back. During the course of our journey into the night the sheets and canvas that obscured her had come away from Irish Jenny's face. She seemed almost luminescent in the dark, with an aura of the faintest blue.

The Bazouk paused for a long moment, then reached around the unfortunate girl's neck. His hands and fingers were so sturdy, had the man worn a wedding ring you might well drop a silver dollar through it, but for all of his savage bulk he was as gentle with the dead girl as a mother might be with a newborn as he unclasped a thin silver necklace bearing a tiny silver cross. He lay the cross on his calloused palm and displayed it to me, before tucking it inside his coat pocket.

Whether he thought it an amulet blessed by death or perhaps some talisman particular to his own foreign ethos I do not know, but it seemed appropriate that something of Irish Jenny remain in the world. That Bashi-Bazouks have a reputation for robbing the dead was well-known, especially if they had been the cause of that death, but I did not think this particular instance to be born of some inbred sense of riot or a predilection for looting.

This memorial act done, he covered the face of the girl with the sheets and then set the paving stones in the canvas tote before threading one of the pieces of rope though the eyelets at the top and cinching it shut. He then took Irish Jenny by the shoulders and motioned for me to take her up by her legs. We walked her to the water and there let her slip into the midnight sea and its concealing darkness. It was just past three in the morning.

We took up our positions in the carriage, and once again the dark-haired woman took up my arm. I directed the Bazouk to take us both to my rooms and she settled into my side. After the dock was a few quiet blocks out of the way I asked for her name.

"Dia," she said, "Dia Fortuna. At least for the last little while. Before that there were others."

I nodded. I have known many people of many names both common and uncommon. To traffic in rare books and the pursuit of illicit sensual pleasures is to move among aliases. Some ridiculous, some sedate.

"Who is Imbroglio?"

She looked up at me and it seemed that of all the strange circumstances of the night only that surprised her – that I did not know of Imbroglio.

"Well, you know sir," she said. "He is of one name only. Imbroglio. He arranges. He procures. He panders. He is known to many, if not recognized by all. He secures such services as you might not speak of, in your fine houses and carriages. Services that are of course common enough, but performed in secret and not to be spoken of aloud. It was he that arranged for me and Irish Jenny to attend the residence at which you found us."

I understood what she was saying of course and had not ever had any doubts as to her hire and from that, her station in life.

"So then," I asked. "What did this Imbroglio tell you about your attendance upon my friend's house – an attendance arranged by his conveyance?"

"Only that a wealthy gentleman required the two of us for an 'experiment' she said. At this she nestled back into my arm again.

I continued my interrogation. "Did you understand the nature of the experiment? Was it explained to you?"

"Not in such details as you witnessed," she said, yawning, "but it was hardly the first time a gentleman of uncertain provenance had arranged for something vaguely described via Imbroglio. We were promised a consideration, in such terms as to make it very hard to say no, and with such an amount on offer my curiosity was either stifled or piqued, I am uncertain as to which. Both are a spur to the partaking in their own way. The first, not to know too much, and the latter, to know it all."

I left it at that until we arrived at the hotel.

"Dia," I said, "I would that you remain under my care for a few hours yet. My suite is comfortable, and secure, and you may garner what rest you can. You may have heard my friend's – the Professor's – instructions to see to it that your agent Imbroglio is paid. I will take care of that. I have two things by which I might provide you security. The Bazouk, of course," I nodded at the ogre driving the carriage, "and more than enough money to buy the connivance of any two Imbroglios. Will you stay?"

She wearily nodded. "I will trust you."

I asked the Bazouk then, if he could arrange for this Imbroglio's attendance upon my suite at six o'clock of that very evening. The Bazouk nodded. He too, bore an air of indifference to the night's events, as if it was all merely part of his regular employ and a night like any other. Had he not been so sentimental in the recovery of Irish Jenny's fragile silver pendant I would have thought him an automaton or beast of burden of some sort, but I had seen what I had seen, and understood why the Professor relied upon him. The man had something of a soul, somewhere.

The Bazouk sent on his way, Dia and I went to my rooms. None of the hotel staff so much as batted an eyelash at us. I was not the first fine gentleman to stay in that establishment, and she not the first whore to cross their threshold in a fine gentleman's company. For them at least, it really was a night like any other.

We gained entry to my rooms where Dia climbed into my bed with no particular grace at all and fell asleep in her clothes ere her head hit the pillow. I removed my jacket and sat in the great chair and set my feet in my boots upon the low table. I unbuttoned my shirt and vest a little and I too was asleep in an instant. The palest blue light came in through the window on the east wall of the suite, dawn had come and started to wash out all of the stars save Venus, who stayed as long as she could before she too, acquiesced to sleep, but only long after we did.

Dia woke me up mid-afternoon. "Might a gentleman provide me with a modest meal?"

I rang for service and in short order a porter appeared. I ordered bread, butter, coffee, boiled eggs, and fruit. In due course the meal arrived and the porter bowed and left us. We ate with our hands and fingers, eating like children eat after going too long without. The fruit in particular was sublime, the juice ran down from our mouths and we both laughed at the immodest sounds we made. I finished first and watched her eat, and she, watching me watch her, smiled.

"You should pay me for that," she said.

"For what?" I asked.

"The pleasure you take in watching me eat."

"You are right," I said. "I should and I will, but I will refrain for a moment. What I will pay you for, if you will have it, is for you to tell me of the Star Flower the Professor set upon you last night, and of your experience of it."

She stood and wiped her mouth carefully with her hand and sucked the last of the fruit's juice from her fingertips. I found this gesture prurient – in the best possible sense. She undressed then, letting her clothing drop to her feet before kicking it away. She then walked to the bed, never taking her eyes from me the whole time, and got in, propping herself up against the pillows. She put the soles of her feet together then, and let her knees fall out, and, after leaving her vulva exposed to me for an all too brief time, patted it with her hand before covering it.

"Look at my eyes, gentleman," she commanded me, and I tried but could not. Again she spoke, this time softly, "Look at my eyes," and I, with all the strength I could muster, did.

She spoke then, softly and carefully, with an apparent consideration for her words. There were none that could be considered careless.

"Before the Star Flower experiment, which the Professor charmingly described to us as 'wearing a unique botanical specimen in such a manner as to obscure your face, while I observe the effects' he allotted us laudanum and brandy. He had, as you probably know, a lot of brandy. I do not pretend to be an expert in brandies, but I know men – gentlemen such as yourselves, set a high stock on the appreciation of its various brands and dates. I did not worry at all about the 'botanical specimen' – in fact I thought he might just want to draw us. This is more common than you think. Men like to talk – and draw – as much as they like more carnal pleasures.

"But in time the soporifics took effect and Jenny and I disrobed and took our places on the tables indicated. There your Professor's enormous manservant bound us with the leather belts fastened to the table. We'd been bound before. As I said, the amount of the consideration provided to Imbroglio for our attendance, and the Professor's assurances as to our safety, and the laudanum, were all satisfactory enough for us to go along with the protocol. I remember that Jenny laughed when the

Professor set the buckles on her ankles – a pure and sweet sound. You could not hear Jenny's laugh but love her, poor girl. I cannot speak for her, but I'd been restrained before, for worse consideration, and in worse company. The sheets upon us – which I thought frivolous, but made no remark upon because, again, the consideration – were drawn up and the men brought the Star Flower, as you no doubt observed."

At this she withdrew her hand slightly from her vulva, parting, with the spread of her middle and index fingers, the labia majora and exposing her softly folded brown labia minora which had, to my eye, begun to glisten.

"My eyes, sir," she said, still speaking softly and deliberately, with the faintest trace of bemusement in her voice.

Gently chastised this way I again looked into her eyes. This time I resolved not to look away, come what may.

"The Star Flower then," she said, "ah, the flower of that elder race. From the moment they placed it on my face I was flooded with sensations all at once arcane and animal. It was wet to be sure, wet like I am now, wet with anticipation of the joy of copulation. It sang to me, in a thousand voices, and it took me. How so you wonder? The Star Flower, in its power, recreated in my body and soul every carnal experience that I had ever had, and all of them – all of them – it recreated at the same time. Can you imagine that?"

I watched her trace the line between her darkening labia minora with a single finger, parting their velvet enticement to show the wet pink of her vagina. Having parted herself so she then rested the tips of her middle and index finger upon the prepuce of her clitoris. She didn't speak again until again I looked up into her eyes.

"Again," she said, "every experience, all at once. Remember, I was not always Dia Fortuna. I was born Magdalena, in what you would call Hungary, under the sign of Venus. We were of the blood of the old Magyars, an ancient and dignified people. I had a mother, and a father too. But we had no land, and no title. We had nothing of anything in the old country. We were little better than serfs. So we came here, to this country. Still, I was not a whore. I was a good girl in the Orthodox fashion. I helped my mother in the garden and in the house, and I prayed diligently.

"My father found work in New York City, among the garment factories. All too soon, he died there, rent to pieces in their machinery. My mother, bereft and unsupported, did what she could for me. Do not suppose anything of this – I still was not yet a whore. She found a position for me in the house of an old New England family, a servant to an old and dignified woman whose husband had been the owner of many great merchant ships. He had been much older than she and she had been a widow twenty years when I joined her household. She governed the fortune he'd left her and busied herself in charity and reverie, running the house with a light hand.

"The household was small. No permanent servants but myself and an Argentinian boy named Alejandro, who was both valet and carriage-man – much like your Professor's man. He undertook her errands, he drove her, he kept the horses, and he was the most beautiful creature I had ever seen."

My eyes had again gone to her vulva. She had now wetted the pad of her middle finger with the lubrication of her vagina and she moved that finger in a slow, circular motion around the circumference of her clitoris. Her labia, dark with arousal now, revealed, at syncopated intervals in the motion of her fingertips, the glistening pink tip of her erect clitoris.

"You may look at me now," she said. "You may look at me however you want to look at me."

There was a subtle catch in her breath when she spoke. I heard it. I knew what that meant. I stood up and took off my vest and unbuttoned my shirt all the way to my waist and walked to the foot of the bed. Had I but dared, I could have reached out and touched her. But I dared not yet, and she continued.

"I began to make love with Alejandro. We'd steal away – to the shed in the garden, to the carriage house, the arboretum too. If we had time, we were naked together, and unashamed. Done, we'd slink away to our duties like feral cats until circumstances allowed us to be together again. At last we grew careless, and one day, while I lay on top of my beautiful Argentinian boy, making love to him with the rhythm of my hips and with the soles of my bare feet warm underneath the back of his calves, our mistress caught us. I was, briefly, and for the only time ever, ashamed.

"Then my mistress spoke to me. 'Do not stop,' she said. 'Continue as you were before I arrived. Pretend I am not here.' The shame left my cheeks and I began to make love to Alejandro with the rhythm of my hips and the fierce strength in my hungry little servant's ass just as I had before my mistress had arrived. I closed my eyes, faster and faster I rode Alejandro, until he could no longer restrain himself and began to tell me he loved me in his sweet Argentinian Spanish with his climax. It was then that my mistress came to stand beside us and ordered me, calmly and without rancor, to stop my movements. I opened my eyes and watched her place the first two fingertips of her right hand in her own mouth. She looked me in the eyes then pulled her wet fingertips from her mouth. With her left hand she reached back to my nice round servant's ass and pulled me ever so slightly farther apart, and then, with those two self-same fingertips she began to trace a circular pattern on my anus. When the pressure of her simulation was increased just enough to penetrate that profane place, I fell – by which I mean I had the sensation in my stomach of rising or falling, of being severed from the pull and security of the earth – I fell so hard into an orgasm that I actually cried.

"Alejandro had come earlier as I had noted, and when we finally uncoupled his semen overflowed from my womb and spilled out of me onto our makeshift couch there amongst the carriages. Done, my mistress walked away without a word. Believe you me, I throbbed. I was still in throes, and the waves of them abated only incrementally. The next day, of course, we did the very same thing. The day after, again – except this time she placed her thumb there, deep inside me where her fingertips had only dared to trace. There were more and more days.

"On a Thursday in August so hot there were reports of people dying in their tenements in the city, I had my mistress kneel naked before me with her face to the floor. I blindfolded her as she instructed and I saw the welts on her shoulders laid there by the cruelty of her long-dead husband and marveled at her resilience. I loved her in that moment. I kissed these welts, and then I kissed the length of her spine and then performed anilingus on her until she too, cried with the relief of orgasm as once had I.

"There are more stories too. There were many days of love like that until she passed away and the household was auctioned off and I finally became a whore. That first day, and all the days after, were all in the kiss of the Star Flower, and all now concurrent with one another, each happening again and again exactly as it had happened the first time."

She arched her back and hips at this, and threw back her head, exactly as she had when in the obscene kiss of the Star Flower, and again seemed to be ascending. She was fully exposed to me then, and flush with pleasure, her labia minora the color of a plum and slick with passion.

"From his lips/Not words alone

pleased her."

I spoke, and with these words begged to join her.

She relaxed her arch and came back to set her eyes on me. I was undressed now and leaning on the bed, exposed at her feet. She asked, "Who said that?"

"Milton," I said, "it's from Paradise Lost."

"Why do you say that," she asked.

"It seemed appropriate to our situation," I said. "I do not know why."

She extended a finger to me and with it, beckoned me to join her, and I lay upon the bed with her. I could smell, in her hair and on her breasts, the faintest scent of the Star Flower from its coupling with her in the Professor's laboratory. I could trace, under her cheek and on her belly, the faintest veins of the mauve hematic that same flower had caressed her with. She embraced me with her hips and her legs and guided me to within her body and I felt the heat from the soles of her feet on my calves just like that lucky Argentinian boy had. I strove, I strove, with all the strength of my bodily passion to possess her like that aggregation of moments provided by the alien flower until eventually I surrendered to her envelopment and spent myself in great, rushing volumes inside her.

We lay there a while, she on her back and I beside her, my arm across her waist.

"That," she said, "was more pleasurable than the attentions of any gentlemen I have ever entertained since the passing of my mistress and the recall of my beautiful boy Alejandro to Argentina. You, sir, are a warrior. So, please don't think it an insult or disparagement from me to tell you that as much as I enjoyed that and want it again even to the point where I might beg – a little – it is not the tenth part of the carnal invocations of the Star Flower. You must believe me."

"I do," I said. Content, I rested a minute then, without any thoughts at all until all at once one intruded with its own knife's edge. I sat up and asked Magdalena:

"Then what happened to Jenny?"

She sighed and looked out at the afternoon light winding around the edges of the drapes.

"I cannot say for sure," she said. "But it's possible that in the sum of her experience of sexual congress before the Professor laid the Star Flower on her face there might not have been any kind and guiding mistress such as I had, nor some dark-eyed and worshipping boy to sing the love songs of the gauchos out on the Argentinian Pampas.

Had her experiences not been so kind as were mine, all of them at once might have caused her so severe a distress as to cause her soul to flee her small, pale body."

"My God," I said, and then again, "My God."

"We might both have been whores," she said, her voice calm and measured, "but we came to it each by our own path and held nothing in common other than our trade."

She did not speak again, and we lay in silence until the shadows grew long.

V: IMBROGLIO

At half past five there was a single knock at the door – not unlike someone attempting to break in using a battering ram. I knew it had to be the Bazouk. I draped myself in a sheet and opened the door for him. He handed me one of the Professor's cards, this marked only with a handwritten "X" and I knew that the man Imbroglio had accepted my invitation.

I told the Bazouk to have the carriage removed to at least some distance from the hotel and then to return with a length of strong but flexible rope and the iron pry-bar kept on the carriage. The bar was of the sort carriage drivers used to lever the carriage up out of road-holes or lift the axle to replace broken wheels, and I'd seen workmen in every city I had ever been to use them in the breaking and moving of concrete sidewalks and pilings. It was an inelegant tool but well-suited to men of brute strength.

The Bazouk spoke no answer aloud but moved off quickly enough, and I presumed upon his understanding. After a shorter time than one would think such a large man needed, he returned with the rope and the prybar and also our canvas tarp. I had not thought of this but the Bazouk, of course, was ahead of me and I understood that he was not the sort of man for whom you had to draw a map. He lay the tarp in the entryway, just inside the door. We then set a table to face the door and two chairs across the table from each other. I set three envelopes upon the table and then secured a noose at one end of the rope. This I set at the floor of the chair facing into the room. I kept the other end of the rope at hand, and very nearly the whole of it was obscured by the table.

I instructed Magda to sit by the window and to turn out all lights save for a single candle which I set upon the table. I had the Bazouk secret himself in the water closet leaving the door so slightly ajar as to not belie any flicker of movement or shadow of his presence.

"You will know what to do and when?" I asked him.

He smiled and gripped the iron bar. It looked to be no thicker than a pencil in his hands.

"He will not come alone," Magdalena said. She bit her lip with anxiety.

I looked at the Bazouk. His face betrayed nothing remotely like concern at this information.

"It is indeed unfortunate for the man who comes with him," I said. And we took our positions.

At quarter past six there came the solemn and measured rap, rap rap of a cane or walking stick at the door. I bade the knocker enter and my visitor pushed the door open with a walking stick and looked around the room, long and hard, ere he stepped in.

Imbroglio, for indeed it could be no other, was not what I expected. He was a dwarf, and lame. He leaned heavily on his stick. He looked to be a son of the Mediterranean coasts of Europe, possibly as Italian as his name to be sure, but possibly of the southern French or even Greek peoples. He had great and luxurious mustachios carefully waxed and curled. His head was shaved and his scalp oiled. Even in the candlelight he gleamed. He wore black trousers, heavy black boots, and a gold waistcoat over a crisply laundered white shirt. He wore a monocle. He was in short, a cheat, a thief, and a pimp now caricatured as a gentleman.

Behind him came a sort of secretary or protector, a lean and sallow type of man, the kind that scours battlefields to dispatch and dispossess the wounded. This man was clean shaven and wore a plain brown wool overcoat over a suit of faded black. It was not cold enough to justify such a coat outside and certainly not inside. The man could only have worn it to conceal a weapon. I invited the dwarf to sit down and his man assisted Imbroglio in removing his coat. I had a brief and fleeting fear that Imbroglio would sit upon the chair and his feet would thereby be too far above the trap I had set for him, but his coat removed he examined the chair and realizing that his chin would hardly clear the edge of the table he elected not to sit.

"I prefer to stand, sir," is all he said, and he stood across from me in the center of the snare I had set.

"Let's not waste your time," I began … but the dwarf, imagining himself to be … just what I don't know, interrupted me by putting a finger to his lips. I stopped speaking. Let him talk I thought. Let him prate.

"I am," he began, "aggrieved."

I would not give him a response.

He gave up waiting for me and began to talk again.

"I am aggrieved," he said. "Last night two of my miggliori puttane failed to return from their designated assignation. Let me assure you, sir, that my concern for them was genuine, and heartfelt. Then, this morning, before I had dressed and before my customary time to take visitors, your man comes to seek an audience with me, and when denied, he proceeded to abuse my friends and employees in order to secure it."

The dwarf looked around the room, looking for the Bazouk. By your man I knew he meant the Bazouk and I admit, the thin crease of smile crossed my lips when I thought of what he might have done in terms of abuse to any one of Imbroglio's henchmen who sought to bar his way, standing in some doorway with their arms crossed across their chest like they were some sort of force to be reckoned with. Some people have no judgment and must learn everything by the most difficult kind of rote.

"The man you speak of is not my man. He is the good Professor's, and he is not here. In the matters before us I am acting as the Professor's agent and that is all."

Although the pompous, monkey-faced dwarf was visibly put out by my interruption, I noted that his man, holding Imbroglio's coat in his arms, seemed to relax a little when I told my lie as to the Bazouk's absence from this premises.

"Nonetheless your man, whoever you are," he said, "had the temerity to tell me that my whore Jenny, Irish Jenny or Dublin Jenny to those of us who cared for her, had been slain at this debauchery of your master's. Slain. I do not think it inappropriate at all to suggest that she was murdered. Who would murder Irish Jenny I have to ask myself? I had offers to sell her into marriage. Fine gentlemen too. Not Professors or agents, but gentlemen. So, who would murder my Jenny, if not to deprive me of the income derived from my valuable chattel? What am I to think?

Did you know that I have a girl from the Sudan – one of the Mahdi's one-hundred and thirteen-odd daughters I like to tell people, because it might not even be untrue – that is as dark as my fair Jenny was light? For the right consideration, for the right gentleman (he spat the world gentleman at me) I could pander them as a pair, and generate the income of a prince? Did you know that? Do not answer me, agent. I know you did not know that. You are an agent, and not the principal. I tell you this for your own good. I should not be so generous."

"Are you done," I asked.

"No sir, indeed I am not," he said. "Not at all. As I said, you have deprived me of the income of princes at the misuse unto death of my property, and then, rather than atone to me properly you send your Professor's uncouth oaf to visit indignities upon my practice and you demand that I attend upon you to discuss the matter of making reparation? You ..."

I stopped him with a waive of my hand. "Dwarf," I said, and again for emphasis "Dwarf. Let me expedite this matter so that I can return to being an actual gentleman and you to being a mere pimp who temporarily finds himself among his betters and becomes momentarily insane enough to forget to be humble."

The dwarf reddened. His face looked like nothing so much as those monkeys of the African plains whose asses redden and swell in the mating season. Rendered apoplectic by my words, he could not speak his ire. Satisfied, I continued:

"There are three matters before us. Firstly, the fair-haired whore named Jenny. All of your aspersions to the contrary, fair Jenny was not that healthy and passed away accidently. Let us not pretend. I know nothing of any pairing with some Sudanese girl of uncertain lineage, although I admit, the idea intrigues me. But that's for another time. Here, in the first envelope (and I slid it to him) is consideration for that loss. Look at it, count it, and accept it without any manufactured argument. It's as good as it will ever be. My God man, the woman is dead. I note that you didn't bother to ask where her body might be, that you may give the poor thing a good, Christian burial. You did not weep that there was no opportunity to hire a priest to come and chant some papist cant and superstition over a good and proper coffin on behalf of her poor lost soul."

I could see his eye twitch with rage behind his monocle and I thought to myself that by God, I'll have that monocle pop out if I have anything. He took the envelope and started to withdraw the money to count it. A grubby little pimp indeed I thought, always and forever.

"There is one-hundred dollars in there," I said. "Think of it as the income due a prince, fair enough, but only of a dwarfish prince, the least of all princes."

He shook with rage.

"The second matter is of course, the lady in the room with us. Whoring is an ancient and honorable profession; but I would advise you not to refer to Dia Fortuna, (at this I turned to her to confirm) as a chattel. You failed to mention it – or just had another overly long grievance prepared that I don't have time to listen to – but she has been in our company overly long versus what you were provided consideration for and as we are gentlemen, and not malformed imps, we therefore would offer you a sum in further consideration for her time, which is to continue until I see fit."

I slid the second envelope to him and said, forcefully, that he should open it perforce. As with the first envelope the moment he began to withdraw the banknotes within I told him, "Put it down. There is one-hundred dollars in there, as with the last envelope. It is now I who must bear your outrageous insults. I have already demonstrated, and proven with the first envelope, that I am more than fair and honest in dealing with these matters."

His eyes had narrowed to slits and, under pressure, his monocle dropped out and like a climber falling down a cliff bounced off of his rage-veined cheeks to land on the table at his hand.

"The third matter then," and I gestured at the third envelope, "is of your lost honor and reputation. Although this conversation could have gone better, you do deserve something for your discretion and a solemn promise not to ever, ever discuss these circumstances of which we have spoken with anyone, ever. Go ahead and open it."

I did not push this envelope to him. I made him reach for it. I thought it possible that he might have to reset his feet to reach it and that they would come off of the floor and out of my snare. Reach he did though, and I knew he was on his tiptoes. I noted that he wore rings, great, gaudy, old woman's rings, on every finger of his preternaturally short hands.

This last envelope I had left void of any content and when he went to draw from it he knew it empty for a certainty, just as I had intended when I first set the envelope out.

"For your honor," I said.

The dwarf could barely draw breath he was so angered.

"Cazzo questo ragazzo," he said to his man, then, "E anche la puttana."

His man moved to whatever weapon he had inside his coat but the Bazouk had already stepped out from the water closet and in two steps was close enough to swing the iron tamping bar in an arc wide enough scrape the walls of my suite. Magdalena ducked. The dwarf's hireling never even got his hands out of his coat when the Bazouk struck him with such force the flat edge of the bar buried itself halfway into the man's cranium. A great pink clot of brain – and one eye – came out as if spewed from a hose and neared the ceiling before conceding to gravity and landing on the startled pimp.

He looked up at the Bazouk in astonishment.

I stood and pulled on the rope surrounding his shoes as hard as I could. The snare worked as intended, and I pulled the angry runt off of his feet. His cane flew some distance away and Magdalena moved from her chair to pick it up. He struggled to gain his feet but I commenced to walk backwards across the room, pulling him along and keeping him on his back. The Bazouk hooked three of his meaty fingers into the seeping brain cavity of the dwarf's dead guard and dragged the body to the canvas on the floor. Imbroglio struggled, but he made no sound at all. His habits, I think, were formed of the illegal and clandestine, and he had been conditioned to hold his silence. He was, in this way, very nearly complicit with me in engineering his own demise. Although he could not ever have imagined himself to be the victim and not the perpetrator, he raised no alarm for any friend, stranger or even a ghost, a devil or an angel to succor him.

At last I had backed to the wall and could drag the pimp no farther. He began to search among his pockets then, and I feared he might have some weapon by which to free himself. My thought was barely complete when the Bazouk stepped over and, seizing the rope where it was the most taut – just before the knot of the noose and within a handspan of the dwarf's feet – lifted Imbroglio into the air. He commenced to shake the little man then, like you would shake a fish on a hook, and all manner of things become dislodged from the pockets of Imbroglio's trousers and vest. A small knife with a wicked hook, a switchblade, a twin-barreled derringer, and a kosh all fell out and rattled on the floor along with a purse from which spilled all manner of silver specie from the mints of a half-dozen nations. Defeated, Imbroglio hung there in the Bazouk's grasp in silence.

"At last he makes no complaints," I said to the Bazouk, then nodded my head.

The Bazouk swung the hapless procurer like a man swinging an anvil on a chain. Once, twice (Magdalena ducked again) and then a third time the Bazouk swung the dwarf footed to the end of the rope in a great revolution around the room until, with the frightening imposition of a fatal momentum, the Bazouk brained Imbroglio against the fireplace, making a sound not unlike that made when dropping an overripe gourd from a four-story rooftop. Although I thought from the initial sound that the fireplace brick had cracked, the brick, accompliced to all of us now, remained stoic and unmarred.

Any potential complications we had with the pimp Imbroglio were now ended. Magdalena stepped over the gore and began to pick up Imbroglio's scattered possessions. The Bazouk methodically lay the dead men side by side on the canvas he'd brought, but then stopped. He'd performed some internal calculi and realized that there was not enough canvas to cover the two. I saw this and went to one of my trunks and emptied it of my clothing.

"We'll put the dwarf in here," I said, and the Bazouk grunted his assent.

In short order both cadavers were stripped – Imbroglio's henchmen had been found only to be carrying a set of brass knuckles and a short knife – no contest at all for a Bazouk armed with a five-foot iron lever, and the dwarf swung from his heels by a length of rope. Before we shut the trunk lid on the morbidly disfigured Imbroglio, the Bazouk, with his experienced looter's eye, reached beneath the dwarf's spattered blouse and pulled out a thick golden chain, with a three-inch long cross of gold displaying an uncut ruby heart on it. His expression was of the deepest satisfaction as he pulled it off of the dead man. He displayed it to me, laying the cross on his palm in much the same manner as he had shown me Irish Jenny's article of faith, and then tucked it into his sash.

I sent the Bazouk out with the dead henchman wrapped in canvas over his shoulder and instructions to bring the carriage to the front of the hotel. That done I took Magdalena to the front desk and, using some of the bank notes from the envelopes with which I'd taunted Imbroglio, paid the front desk and made arrangements to have my possessions, including a dead dwarven panderer in a trunk, delivered to the foyer of the hotel to be loaded onto the carriage by the Bazouk when he arrived.

I tipped the porter twenty dollars to see that the room be cleaned in such a manner as that I did not have to hear about its state ever again. I also arranged for a suite of rooms at a different hotel. Although I doubted Imbroglio had any of the sort of friends who might seek to avenge him, you can never be too sure, and experience had taught me that a quick and subtle change of direction was often a worthwhile discretion.

The three of us, exhausted and silent, sat in the carriage, but this time Magda sat in the front seat beside the mighty Bazouk. I understood then in light of what had just happened, and in anticipation of a storm to follow, she might seek the shelter of the mightiest tree in the forest. I sat beside her on her other side. The Bazouk, from whom I had never seen much in the way of sentiment, took the reins in his right hand and with his left reached all the way across his body to tousle Magda's hair and she leaned against him.

"Come Bashi Bazouk," she said, "Tell me your name."

"I have had many," he said, with not much of an accent, "and because of that now I will have none."

I marveled to hear him speak. I had assumed him either mute, or monumentally stoic. At one time I had even thought that his tongue must have been torn out for some indiscretion in the palace of Topkapi, or some other Despot's den of iniquity. The man's comportment lent itself to all manner of wild speculation.

"Your English is very good, sir," I told him. Tell me, how is it that I have never before heard you speak?"

"You never spoke to me," he said.

Fair enough, I thought.

"As for my English," he said, "I rowed at Oxford."

Both Magda and I started.

"Not really," he said, laughing broadly at our surprise. "Not at all. But it gets them every time and now I have you, too. I have Russian too, and Turkic and Arabic, a little French and less German."

We laughed at that and for the briefest of moments we were able to forget about the rendered bodies on the cart behind us.

"Tell me then, Bashi," Magda said. "What of your people? Do you have a mother? A father? A home and a place?"

"A mother?" he asked. "Only the briefest of memories. Memories so short I think they might be dreams or wishes. A father?" He shrugged. "None but war and war alone, my father is. A home and a place? No home. Of that I can be sure. I am of those people called Circassian by others, and of the tribe of the Zhaney in our own language, now scattered and disposed by a line of Tsars, a succession of Sultans, and a thousand other lesser evils. A place? What is that? My place is where I stand, or, in this instance, where I sit. My service to the Professor is as much of a place as I have ever had. It suits me. One tires of perpetual war no matter how much one loves it. War is the father who can never be satisfied. War is the son who strives to please his father forever.

"That is unfortunate," Magda said. "All people should have a home and a place. After those things there are only ever situations, or nothings. I think that I have fallen in the world. I have gone from my father's and mother's home, to a place within my mistress's house, and then when that was gone I came into a situation with Imbroglio. Now that he is gone, I will have to find another situation. So, you see how I have fallen. I have fallen to nothing. My aspirations are only to another situation, and not a place, and I do not even dream of a home. Such things are for other, luckier people."

The Bazouk, moved by this, reached carefully to within his blouse and withdrew one of the many talismans he wore, the most recent examples of which were the charms he had taken from Irish Jenny and Imbroglio. This one was of tarnished silver, a coin on a leather thong. He took it off and handed it to Magda.

"Here, little bird," he said, "I believe that it still has much luck in it."

Magda, beaming, took it in her hand and lay it on her palm to show me. It was a roman denarius from the time of Marcus Aurelius. Valuable to a collector, but the Bazouk had obviously kept it on his person a long while. Whatever he had come to, he had never looked to sell it.

"Thank-you, Bashi," Magda said, "thank you. How came you by this? What luck shall I expect?" She let the thong slip around her head and settled the coin just below the hollow of her throat.

The Bazouk leaned back and spoke. "I do not know the date of my own birth, so I cannot speak certainly to my own age, nor of the year I found the talisman, but I think I was about sixteen years old. I had already taken up arms, as had many of my Circassian brothers-in-exile, and we served in the Sultan's wars against the Bulgars. Bashi-Bazouk means headless in the language of the Ottomans, meaning we had no formal leader. Each man is his own man. We drew no wage, and none would be offered. Instead we imposed our will by arms and took our pay in spoil, each man looking only unto himself.

"We burned empty villages one by one. We offered battle but were given none. The Bulgars harassed us by bolt and bullet from the high places then withdrew, hoping to starve us out. Their strategy was sound. Soon enough we hungered in the rain that poured in the mountain passes. At last we came to a village, prosperous enough by the look of it, and a short battle was joined. The result was inconclusive, and we were in no position to take up a siege. Our mood was foul. Men murdered each other in duels for the last of the rations we had brought with us. Men boiled and ate grass.

"The Ottoman general who assembled us offered a false truce to the Bulgars to parley with us, and when they sent their Voivode and his hetman out to negotiate, he instructed us to seize and impale them alive and set their writhing bodies on the field before the gates, which we did perforce. Mayhem ensued. The last of the Bulgars came out of the gates with all their arms, and at last battle was joined. They should have waited out our provocations, and let hunger disband us. They were few and we were many, and the matter was decided quickly. They were slain in the melee, or their throats slit and their heads cut off if they offered surrender.

"Then, while the slain bled and the wounded wept, the plunder commenced. We raced through the town with our swords in our hands and holding firebrands. When they locked themselves in their church, we burnt the church and all inside. If we found them hiding in their cellars, we dismissed all pleas and bribes. They were dragged out and slain. The injured we threw screaming into the same fires as the dead. The women and children somehow still alive were rounded up and taken to the field of the impaled and ordered to undress. It was the habit of the Bulgar women to hide their specie and jewelry by sewing it into their dresses and pleats, and the clothing itself was worth something if not bloodied. This action was done quickly and without ceremony and then we killed them all.

"None were left lying with their heads still joined to their bodies. Ears were cropped, and fingers taken for trophies too. All night long the fire of the church burned and burned, if you were close enough to it you would think that it was noon from the heat and light.

"The next morning we scoured the village in small groups or, in my case, alone, looking for any cellar unopened, or hoping to see the glint of anything valuable to carry off in the ashes of the remains of any house or shop. There were none but the dead to constrain us, and the dead can impose nothing. We had killed them all. I had come across a black horse, a fine and healthy animal, and laid claim to it. It would be the first horse I ever owned. I was, by the standards of the Bashi-Bazouk, about to be a rich man.

"I led the horse by a rope through the streets when I saw a door in the floor of burnt out hovel open upwards, and from the slit of its opening, through a veil of soot, a small boy looked out at me. At once I strode to the door and flung it open and there, unblinking in the light, a boy of five or six years of age stood shivering. He was dark of hair but fair of eye, a beautiful child, and if we weren't committed to murdering every last Bulgar in the village, I thought he'd bring me more money than the horse if I could somehow get him to the slave markets of the Ottomans. How he survived the heat of the fire that consumed his hovel I do not know, but there he was.

"I wrenched him roughly from his hiding spot but he made no cry or complaint. There I saw, around his neck, that same silver coin I have just given you now. I spit into the ashes that surrounded us and it hissed – that's how hot the remains of the fire were. A miracle of some sort I thought, some strange bit of luck for the Bulgar boy. I wrapped the boy from head to toe in one of my travel-blankets and lay him across the croup of the horse and walked him out of town and there, away from the eyes of my blood-brothers I let him go.

"Not even I can tell you why. I am blooded in war; my body now bears over seventy wounds. I have never prayed and I hold to no superstition. Indeed, I have boasted that I have made many ghosts, but feared none. Whatever it was that moved me, I let the boy go by the tree line and told him only to run and never look back. He took three steps, then took off the coin and gave it to me. I never saw him again. I have thought upon it, and I don't think it mere superstition to say the coin saved the boy and that someday it might save me. I thought as long as the boy lived, the coin would keep me alive. I believe he still lives. I give it to you now and it is my belief that it will bring you to your place, and perhaps even to your home."

Magda leaned against the big man then, her head against his great shoulder, and he in turn leaned into her. I thought to myself that I might advise the Bazouk that belief in luck was in itself to hold a superstition but I thought that of all superstitions luck might be the most likely to be true, and I held my words within me. I felt myself apart from them then, my family fortune having ensured that I would never know want of home or place, and that there was no situation that I could think of that would ever be beyond my contrivance. To come to nothing? I could not even imagine it.

We rode the remainder of the way in silence, Magda fingering her gift over and over, and soon enough we were at new rooms. I dispatched the Bazouk back to the Professor, leaving the mangled corpses in his charge on the carriage in their trunk and canvas roll respectively. I told the Bazouk we'd commit them to the sea just as we had done with the late Jenny but we'd wait until the dead of night to do that. He understood. I once again summoned a porter and ordered some sort of a meal for Magdalena and, exhausted, we collapsed in chairs and waited for it to come.

"Did you have to kill Imbroglio and his man?" she asked me.

"No," I told her. "I did it because I wanted to."

"I do not understand," she said.

Here I note that whatever Magdalena said, she always said it with the same low and measured tones. Her voice was always of the timbre of conspiracies planned and undertaken in the bedroom, made from the understanding that what was ever to happen, to listen was to consent, and to consent was to abet. She could have sold sand to a Bedouin. I belonged in psyche and soul, to her voice.

"You did not tell me he was a Dwarf," I said. "I had expected someone more menacing, and less mendacious."

"He had a large personality," she said. "Imposing in his own fashion. He had survived a long time for one so afflicted from birth."

"Indeed, he had," I said. "And although I had not met him prior, from the moment he walked in I knew who he was, and how he had come to mediate your arrangement with the Professor."

She arched an eyebrow and I continued.

"When I first heard of him, he was not Imbroglio. Rather he was spoken of as Poivre. That is another ridiculous name – it is "Pepper" in English. He claimed to be French Canadian, a courier de bois and late of the fur trade. He was a purveyor of flesh then, too, and that's how the Professor knew him. You went to the Professor, there in his laboratory, and saw the great collection of flora at his disposal and assumed him to be nothing more than an old man a little too committed to a particular hobby. But let me tell you of how I know the Professor.

"He is a Medical Doctor of the finest quality, a very learned man, and an instructor of Medicine at the university. I was his student at one time. As part of his duties as an instructor he from time to time needed to procure cadavers for dissection and instruction. Poivre – now apparently known as Imbroglio – was his man for such procurements. Imbroglio might have sold Dia Fortuna and Irish Jenny alive, and taken his commission accordingly, but Poivre would have sold you both dead, too.

"It is well we let that poor girl slip into the sea. It is more dignified to rest in the darkness and fall away to quiet nothing than to bear the anatomist's scalpel and be rendered to halves, then quarters, then less than that, and to be mocked by the prurient whispers of some raucous medical students, eventually to wind up a skull on some phrenologist's shelf, or a uterus in a briny jar, while the rest is consigned to an incinerator."

"I had no idea," she said, "but even then, you would not trust to his discretion?"

"I would not," I said. "Whatever I paid that popinjay little pimp, he would have come back for more. Eventually. And he'd have waited until I was gone and attempted to pursue his graft with Professor, who, at his age, is not as able as I am to manage these things. Even so I had not set myself upon killing him – and the clueless bodyguard – until he silenced me with that finger to the lips, as if I was somehow his inferior, and must bear his chastisement. He forgot his station. I abhor a man who misrepresents himself. For that I had him killed."

"What is your name?" She asked.

I told her and she recognized it.

"I wonder that I might know your father," she said.

"You do not know my father," I said. "Of that there is no chance, at all."

She laughed, then sighed. "I need to return to my rooms. All of my clothes are there, and such possessions as I have. I am dispossessed it would seem. I am not Dia Fortuna anymore."

I gave her the remainder of the money from the envelopes I had taunted the dwarf with. I told her, "Do for yourself as you see fit. By this time tomorrow Imbroglio's disappearance will be presumed upon by every whore and hireling he has. They'll leave their stations in twos and threes, like they have always talked about, and disappear into the streets and rooming-houses of this and a great many other cities. Within a week there will be a new, and perhaps better-named, Imbroglio, with new whores and fresh hirelings. Nature – even the basest nature – abhors a void. Your possessions, whatever they are, will be the property of others and long gone by this time tomorrow. This is the least I can do for you, and I am willing to do more. That Dia Fortuna no longer exists is true," I said, "because from the moment you told me you were Magdalena, I resolved to do whatever I could for you. Here is where I start."

"Then you start late," she said, "Having deprived me of my station before, and not after, bestowing your gifts. So it always is with men like you, for whom money is an endless weight of cure, and not once the smallest proportion of prevention. Having broken, you condescend to buy, and balm your conscience with the unspoken phrase 'I do not have to do this, but I will' and when you say it you think you are speaking a divine truth, and not the taunt that it really is. I cannot even pretend to refuse you, for pride or appearance, because I am no position to do so, and will now probably always be in no position to do so. This is the world's axis, then, for you to play at being generous, and for me to be slave to the pretense."

I thought to argue with her, but I could see, if only in the sadness of her countenance, the truth of what she spoke, or at least how she believed the truth to be. Even had I sought to argue truth with her, a thing to which I was not inclined by nature, I understood the rules of society, which are the truths we live by, whether we will or no, and I knew whereby she had come to her conclusions.

"Forgive me for being careless," I said, "But do not think me callous, at least not by my own design. I know you have not come to take, and that you are no thief. I only offer what I have, which is money. If I do wrong by you, it not because I am trying to do wrong. Forgive me that much."

She looked away before starting back and kissing me then, sucking on my lower lip, putting her arms around me. In the taste of her mouth I caught the faintest wet and floral scent I remembered from the laboratory and the Star Flower. I thought of how she had described her time with her mistress and the Argentinian boy. Each new day built on the foundation of exploration from the one before, and so a tower was built and each new apex was a marvel, to be wondered at but not spoken of for fear that to speak of it was to stop it and to stop it would be to watch it fall.

It was that way with us, too.

VI: TANGIERS

We woke up the next morning in each other's arms and it was some time before we spoke.

"If you could," she said, "would you accept the embrace of the Star Flower?"

"No," I said.

"Ah," she said, in her low, sweet voice, "so you have suffered?"

"No," I said. I thought to distract her by making a joke of it. "It's just that, given my history, and the permissions a great sum of money has allowed my great appetite for deviance to experience – I would surely explode. Then there would be no one to pay the porter to clean up the mess."

She laughed and then turned serious, "So then, if you have not suffered, perhaps you have made others suffer, and it is shame that stays your curiosity."

I looked at her for a long time. In the post-coital reverie of the night before I'd dreamt of the tendrils of the Star Flower, sticky and thrilling, moving through each of us in turn, and binding us to one another. When they moved within me the sensation was not unlike the caress of many hands, and the scent again sublime. I wondered that I had not been dreaming and that my love-making with Magdalena had allowed some residual of the flower to take up residence in me too. I thought of – and discarded the idea in the same instant – the lambskin condoms I had somewhere in my luggage. I hated them and if somewhere the Star Flower had grasped me through Magdalena so what? That was the price to pay.

I decided to confess.

"Tangiers," I said, and she listened. "A few years ago I decided to travel to Tangiers, where the French and a few others have gone to indulge in Persian hashish, fuck hairless young men on the cheap, and indulge in such other recreation as the alleys off of the souks and bazaars can provide."

Once again, Magdalena leaned back on her pillows, and, holding the soles of her feet together with her knees apart like she had the first time, she exposed her vulva to me but this time she did not conceal it under her palm. Rather, she put her fingers in her mouth, after sucking on them slowly and with much saliva she withdrew them to move down to her labia and began to stimulate her prepuce again, concealing then exposing her clitoris in a slow and careful motion.

I looked her in the eyes and continued with my story.

"I made the acquaintance of the various Imbroglios of Tangiers. None of them were dwarves, but all of them were the same sort of merchant. Any vice could be had. I had money of course, but such things as you would not believe could be had in Europe, no matter your purse, were easily arranged in Tangiers. The Imbroglio I had most come to rely on, who went by the name Tahir Sayi – literally "Bad Influence" – had, upon canvassing me for my wants, discovered that I most desired to fornicate with twins, and that I was willing to pay well for the experience of such a night. He said he could provide just that thing.

"A time and a place were set, and at the appointed hour I attended. I knocked on the door and was bidden enter. There, among the rugs and couches were two dark-eyed houris, veiled, robed, and painted with henna like new brides. A massive hookah pipe, the largest I'd ever seen, was set against one wall and bubbled languidly. There was a profusion of hashish on hand. It was so black and sticky you would think it came from the river Styx itself, and it was offered up in an unlimited amount."

Magdalena stopped the rhythm of her wet fingers on her clitoris for a moment and took a deep breath through her nose, then took her labia minora – again the color of overripe brown plums in their excitement – in between the forefinger and thumb of each hand and pulled, teasing each to their modest length and separating them enough for me to see how they shone with her excitement.

"We smoked the hashish in turns." I said, "and the one houri sang to me in Arabic. I knew almost nothing of the language of course, but nonetheless I remember the song as being very pleasant to the ear. Some tribal love-song from the interior I imagine, some lyric about some boy or some girl having eyes like stars and a bottom like a peach and the prospect of love and marriage and sex. In due time we began to kiss, the singer and I at first, then the other twin and me. We did this in turns. They even kissed each other, wetly and heavily, for my amusement."

I stopped my story to move to the side of the bed where I could lean in and kiss Magdalena. I could hear the soft and insistent sound of her fingers on the wetness of her labia and I kissed her hard and deep and without looking I could feel her legs straighten involuntarily as she began to climax.

"Keep going," she said.

"I undressed the singer save for her jewelry and veil, which was all she wore other than the kohl around her eyes and the henna on her hands and feet. I remember how petite she was, and how dark her hair was. I lay her on her back on the cushions, raised her legs by placing her heels in the palms of my hands, and entered her gently. I was in a sea of hashish and lust, and I remember thinking only that I wanted this to last, that I did not want to give up my issue too quickly. It was not that I wanted to 'get my money's worth' – not at all. I could afford the liaison a hundred times if it could be found. I wanted it to last. In order to stop my pending explosion, I took the singer and set her on her knees and entered her from behind. Abi', abi', abi', she said, over and over again. My God she was wet, and it felt at least as good as when she was on her back.

"The other twin meantime, had stepped back to disrobe and then knelt behind us, cupping my scrotum in both hands and gently pulling on it while I thrust in slow regular measures, burying my shaft all the way to carefully cupped scrotum on entry, and then pulling out far enough to see half the head of my phallus, stopping briefly and thrusting again. It was all too good. I'd never spent better money. This second whore then stood up and, disrobed, came to the side of the singer and I, bending over to kiss me full on the mouth, kissing me hot and wet and with a sense of intention I felt could not be faked. The kiss lingered, then the young man – for he was a young man – stood up and I saw his flaccid penis there between his legs.

"I looked up at him and into his kohled eyes and I could see that he was afraid, afraid that his revelation might cost him his consideration, and the singer's too, or even get him maimed or killed. He understood that we had now reached the point where I understood that I had not received what I had paid for. That I abhor misrepresentation I have already told you.

"I stopped my rhythm with the singer and fixed my eyes on the hairless boy in front of me, then uncoupled from her and ordered him, by gesture, to assume her position. She lay to the side of him closest to the hookah and commenced to draw upon the hashish while I squatted behind the nervous boy and spread his ass with both my hands. He, or they, (for I presumed there were attendants involved to present him as the twin of an actual woman), had no doubt sugared him and then plucked with tweezers every hair from his scrotum, perineum, and anus. I paused a moment, my phallus still slick from the copulatory embrace of the singer, then entered him violently. He cried out – Abi' Biltf 'Abi' Biltf – just as she had, only he was frightened. I stared unblinking at the singer – she would not meet my gaze. The young man covered his faced with his hands, and his tears came out from underneath them. But he had been bought and paid for and he endured what only he must. At last I finished in a rage as he reached over to hold the free hand of the singer in his. She looked away then, from he and I both, removing her hand from his and she drew again on the stygian hashish in the hookah.

"I dressed and left them without looking back. I went to my rooms and thought only of my humiliation. And yes, lest I misrepresent myself, I know, that in spite of any excuse I can muster, I sodomized that poor youth because I wanted to. Thus, my pretension of rage at he, his partner, and his procurer."

"Lie here with me," Magdalena said, and she reached out to draw me down beside her.

"There's more," I said. She continued to hold my hand. I was grateful for that, and for the sound of her voice, which soothed me.

"The next day I found Tahir Sayi in one of the bazaars and proposed a recurrence of the previous night's scenario. Although I worried what the whores might have said to him upon their return, he was not at all reluctant to pander to me again. He told me that he knew I would be pleased with his offering, and that he had hoped to make the same arrangement for me again. Tahir Sayi, I imagine, had arranged all manner of things, for lesser or greater sums of money. The 'twins' would come to entertain me again, and he took great pains to assure me that they had been impressed with me and wanted nothing more than to return to my company. I would ordinarily say that a man such as Tahir Sayi need not flatter me, but it was well that he did. Had I heard condescension in his tone, I would have had to take measures against grift, for with men like Sayi the one always precedes the other.

"A runner fetched me after sundown and led me, by many paths, back to the same room that I had met the two in before. He asked, politely but insistently, that he be allowed to search me for weapons. I let him, then entered the room. The girl and the catamite were waiting. The boy betrayed no sign that he had thought anything of the previous night to be anything averse to his person, and the girl, to judge from the expression in her eyes, was at least an hour into the hookah and the most fecund black hashish to be found in Tangiers. I told the girl to sit in the corner and to sing the same song or songs as she had on the previous evening. I told her that she was only to sing, and she was to watch, but not to touch.

"The girl began with her old, tribal verses. There was no pretense of affection, and no languid kissing. I ordered the young man to undress himself. He did this artlessly, looking at the floor the whole time. I shook my head. 'Not good enough,' I said. 'Do it again' Firmly I commanded him. I made him dress, then undress, three times. The girl sang and drew on the black hashish on the hookah. The catamite, nervous at the repeated orders to undress and then dress again asked me questions in a language I did not understand. Finally, he motioned towards the hookah, for indeed, that was what he as asking for. I nodded my assent. He drew upon that most wonderful soporific while his "sister" sang. At some point I ordered him to the cushions and he lay carefully on them and covered his face with his hands. 'No,' I said. 'On your hands and knees, like last night.' He obeyed, rolling over and settling on to his knees with his small, boyish ass in the air.

"The girl looked away while she sang. Her eyes were very brown, almost black. The hashish I thought, it has changed the hue of her irises to match its own abyssal darkness. I marveled at it. The boy kept his face in his hands. I undressed and entered him gently then, not at all like I had the evening previous, and he was warm and incitingly soft like the night before. I counted to ten under my breath – ten strokes, in as deep as I could go, but not forcefully, and out almost to the end of my phallus before thrusting again. There was no Abi', abi', abi' this time, no sound at all except for the shallow intake of his breath and the girl's singing.

"At 'ten' I removed myself from him again and, just as the girl had begun to sing a new song, one she had not sung the night before, I rose up and ejaculated on his back with my hands upon his hips. I came in spasms, insensate of anything but my ecstatic convulsions. The boy arched his back and exhaled loudly. Ai, he sighed, then Aii! I told him to look at me – look at me – but I had surpassed the limit of his English and he remained kneeling, his face down to the ground now, his cheek upon one of the pillows.

"Done, I lay back upon the cushions across from them. The boy began to dress but I remonstrated that he should not do so. They understood, and each drew their knees up against their chests and sat across from me, looking to see when I might dismiss them. I could not, by dint of any Arabic that I had – which was very little – entice them to hold hands. It perturbed me. 'See,' I told her, 'he doesn't want to hold your hand.' She commenced to sing again.

"The rest of the evening passed with my asking them as to their comfort and they shaking their heads because they did not understand me. The hookah bubbled away like the ticking of a clock. The girl actually fell asleep for a while. The boy asked only for the hookah.

"The next day I did not seek out Tahir Sayi, but he found me in the early afternoon. He asked as to my appointments for that evening. I dismissed him rather curtly, saying that I was occupied on business particular to my financial interests and that I would contact him if ever I needed to speak to him again. Of course, I sent a runner from my hotel at nine pm to ask if he could avail me of the young man again.

"And so I began to pass my evenings in Tangiers, each evening in the same manner, indulging, for a premium, in hash and sodomy. I became, in my own mind, a caricature of those Frenchmen who habituated Tangiers in those days, living on the cheap and believing that all things are permissible – how should I put this – looking for a wife, but not in the conventional sense."

Magdalena was still holding my hand. She said nothing, but leaned into me and kissed my shoulder, and ran her fingers through my hair.

"Does this boy you loved have a name?" she asked.

"I never asked," I said. "Nor I did I love him. Not like you ask anyways. In time, I tired of my pursuits – or more accurately, I wearied of looking at myself in the mirror. True, I indulged him as I would a lover, and not a prostitute, by buying him gifts and giving him money. I spoke rarely to Tahir. The boy would come to the door, I would grant him entry to my rooms, and once a week I paid Tahir. Every day I struggled, the half of me that would admit to nothing against the other half craving that boy's smooth, tight ass and wanting to shout for it, to demand that all others see what I saw in his kohled up brown eyes, as dark as his "sister's" but so much less hard. I sought only to be pleasured, he sought only to please. Where you speak of love I thought of ownership, I wanted to be seen as owner. I imagined that my preference for him, and the money derived thereby, had made him something in Tahir Sayi's world. He became as a princeling of some sort in that low society, and had some status denied to the rest of them. I had become, by any standard you can think of, pathetic."

"And still, you did not ask his name?" Magdalena said.

"Never did I ask his name", I said. "I called him only 'Boy'. Soon, I tired of myself in this matter, this dishonest pursuit. When I left the hotel, I left on no notice, and did not reach out to Tahir Sayi, or the boy, and I was scrupulous about not leaving any forwarding information. I left, and when I left, I was gone. I intended to be a ghost. And so, I lost myself for awhile in the capitals of Europe and on the nearer shores of the Mediterranean. But still, in quiet times, or at such times as I heard a woman or girl singing in some foreign tongue I had not ever heard before, my mind turned to Tangiers.

"Eventually I hired a man, 'boots on the ground' so to speak, to make some inquiries. Start with Tahir Sayi I said, Bad Influence as he is known, or at the lower end of the streets, in the hotels and souks that pander to those types of French men that I spoke of. Look for a boy, I said, small but well made, possibly in the company of a young woman, possibly being passed off as brother and sister, and maybe even twins. It took my hireling no time at all of course. Tahir Sayi remembered the boy, and he remembered me. The girl unfortunately, had passed away. Tahir Sayi did not say as to how this had come to occur, only that the lives of those that pass through his are by nature bright and short. Like falling stars that fall upon the water, he said, bright in their own light and the reflected light from the water, but only for a moment, then they are lost. The boy was indeed grieved upon my departure, and had looked for me. I was a good client, kinder than many Tahir Sayi said, and the boy had held an attachment.

"My hireling asked for the boy's name, but Tahir Sayi, a veteran of such negotiations, would not offer it up. He wanted money, a great deal of it. He said that to procure was one thing, but acting as marriage-broker was another. He knew what I was looking for, even if I did not, and he wanted to get paid accordingly. I had foreseen this. I also note that the condescension that Tahir Sayi had theretofore avoided had come to pass. "Marriage broker?" He had gone too far, but I was prepared for this too. The sum of money that Tahir Sayi asked for the boy's name was in excess of the sum I had paid my hireling to garrote Tahir Sayi should they be unable to reach terms and so it was ended. I was left without the boy's name, and Tahir Sayi was forever unable to reveal mine, now that he was just another decomposing body wrapped in chains at the bottom of the harbor.

"Those nights in Tangiers, the hot and still air, the black hashish, the singing of old songs, and the guilty pleasure in the hire, if only for a short time, that wonderful body and the instinct to please, all of it is gone."

"I see," Magdalena said. "Such are our memories of young men, beautiful in their youth, but the time is fleeting. You with your falling star of the desert, and me with my Argentinian groom. All too soon gone, and forever beyond recovery. It is the law of the stars, I think, ancient and unmovable."

"A man – a gentleman – may refuse any gift offered," I said. "But no gentleman destroys that gift so that no one else may benefit of it, and makes such a display of himself doing so. So, no Star Flower for me you see. Not on my own behalf, because there are a hundred, if not a thousand, filthy recurrences I would spend any amount of money on to have all at once, including that of these last pair of days. But I am reminded that I might be of the experiences of poor Jenny, or some other Jenny, in some other place, and I deem myself low."

"You need not worry now," Magdalena said. "Just as I am no longer Dia Fortuna, you are no longer the roué in Tangiers. We do become other people, whether we will or no, and it is not always for the worse."

I stood up. "All of what you say is true. But for now, you need to clothe yourself, and I need to discuss with the Professor his experiments – and the dangerous company he keeps with such as Imbroglio."

We dressed then, without further conversation, and left the hotel separately from one another. I arranged a carriage to the Professor's, and that is where I went.

VII: CHIMERA

When I went to the Professor's place no one answered the door. I was uneasy at the silence in the house and circled the property until I could let myself in. I crossed the lawn that separated the house proper from the laboratory and there, in the laboratory, I found the Professor at a long table covered in the paraphernalia of his science and papers strewn in no particular order that contained the ciphered notes of his research.

He greeted me with only a half-nod or I should have thought he had not seen me at all. I noted the Bazouk asleep on the couch against one wall. It was odd to see the giant in repose, his Safa-style turban that must have had at least eighty feet of cloth to it, lay somewhat askew. The man seemed never to rest, nor to tire from even the severest hard labor, and yet there he was like a child.

I sat across from the Professor and waited for him to speak. Interposed between were some bell jars, each of which contained a large brown spider. This was new to me, and I wondered where he had found them. The Professor noted my curiosity and only then did he speak.

"Phoneutria Nigriventer," he said. "I had some specimens delivered by a former colleague. Phoneutria is better-known as the 'Brazilian Wandering Spider.' Their venom kills its victim by inducing priapism – prolonged and exquisitely painful priapism. Death by erection. Should a native fall prey to the bite of the wandering spider they will lay him upon his funeral bier and bring the women of the village to him, one by one in turn, to assuage this affliction until he is either exhausted of its affects – which can be determined by even the most casual eye as you can imagine – or he expires, whichever is first. I am advised that he usually expires."

I moved my finger to the glass, to gain one of the Phoneutria's attention and it reared back, exposing it's black and white underbelly, and an impressive set of fangs.

"What happens to a woman if she is bitten?" I asked.

"She dies," the Professor said.

He volunteered no further information, and instead began to sort through his notes. I again waited a little before speaking.

"Herr Professor," I said. "What have we done, here, in the laboratory, in this city, over the past two days?"

He did not answer. Instead, he separated the loose papers he had assembled and produced for me a quire containing what I thought must be two dozen or more pages, he'd removed it, it seemed, from the expensive Pharmacopeia I had given him not quite two full days ago. The book was his to do with what he liked, but I could not help but wonder why he had defaced such a valuable acquisition. I could not have ever imagined him doing such a thing.

"The answer is in the book you gave me," he said. "Or, more accurately in this index. It is the key to the cipher."

I did not understand, and my expression gave this away without me speaking.

"The Pharmacopeia – in its most important ciphers, buried here and there among the nonsensical which composes most of the manuscript – describes the creation and perpetuation of what you and I would call a Chimera. A Chimera, by definition, is a hybrid of two different species. A monster, if you will. Minotaur are

Chimera, as are centaurs, satyrs and fauns. These are all examples from pagan myth, and, if you are not in the habit of reading your Bible, I'd suggest you take it up again and see the Book of Genesis wherein is written the story of the Nephilim."

He quoted from Genesis to me then, from memory, as follows:

> 'When people began to multiply on the face of the ground, and daughters were born to them, the sons of God saw that they were fair; and they took wives for themselves of all that they chose. Then the Lord said, "My spirit shall not abide in mortals forever, for they are flesh; their days shall be one hundred twenty years." The Nephilim were on the

earth in those days—and also afterward—when the sons of God went in to the daughters of humans, who bore children to them.'

I gave no indication that I understood anything of what he said, but I did remember, as a former student of his, some of his terminology. I could remember nothing of the Book of Genesis. I cannot remember reading it although I think it might have been one of my father's favorites which is probably why I avoided it.

He continued: "I might say, were I a theologian, that it might be worth arguing Chimera are less monsters than they are angels, given their divine provenance. That is something we can digress to at another time. What I mean to tell you now is this: I have known for some time that the Star

Flower is a hybrid of sorts, a Chimera, and one that lives in stages. I could not advance its stages because I did not know how. Now, thanks to the Pharmacopeia, I do."

"What of the girls?" I asked. "Were you trying to have them, through oral copulation with the Star Flower, bear the next iteration of the Chimera?"

"Yes," he said. "Of course."

I thought him leading himself into madness, in bounds and not steps, and I dared not speak.

"Here," he said, "it's in the book. A Chimera made of two species runs the risk of running out of one species or the other, and thus ending. It is the cardinal rule of life, all life, the lives of men, gods, and Chimera too, that life must go on. Life exists to make more life. It is the tautology we exist by. The Chimera – this Chimera in particular – cannot, so to speak, put all of its eggs in one basket. You saw what happened to the frailer girl. The Chimera's generative process killed her. Had all of it's efforts been placed into her it too, would have ended."

I understood at once it seemed. I had reached for and found a terrifying clarity. I asked him, "It joined her not to inseminate her, but to harvest from her, am I correct?"

"Yes," he said, and he seemed very pleased. "The Chimera sang its ancient song, released its cloying scent, and sent its ethereal tendrils into the women not to sow, but to reap. The Chimera, in its arcane lovemaking, extracted each and every ovum that the woman possessed. From that moment forward they surrendered their children to the Chimera to incubate – for a thousand years if necessary – until such time as it can generate a new life. Those women will not bear any children now, not even one

– but it is quite possible they will be mother to a great many. Innumerable even."

When did you become lost, I thought? "Why harvest the ova of these poor women then, and not the semen of men? It would seem to be far easier to come by the latter than the former."

"Mostly because the archives up to this point – and he pointed at the Pharmacopeia – said so," said the Professor. "It seemed logical. After all, ova are expensive, and protected within the reluctant sex, meted out only at intervals prescribed at creation. The world abounds in semen, but it seems unrefined for the purpose. Believe you me, as far as the donation of ova went, I asked, but could find no volunteers, thus the retention of Master Imbroglio. There was a cost, to be sure, but I don't know what I would have done without him. I've been barred from the university now."

He looked away from me when he said this. It was the first time I thought him shamed by his experiment.

"Of the ova," I continued, "Why the oral copulation? Why not something more genital? Something conventional?"

"Observe the Star Flower," he said. "Their appearance is positively vaginal – vulvular if you will – and in no examination I performed could I find anything approximating penetrative genitalia such as the males of our species exhibit. I managed to perform some experiments," he said, "and determined that much. No, the ova must be harvested – specifically from a living ovulator – at least at the initial stage of gestation."

The query had formed in my mind but I could not, would not ask it aloud, but he saw me and knew my thoughts and answered anyways.

"Yes," he said. "We tried. I had a man Poivre, he was called at the time, although he has had many names, with some expertise in these procurements. He obtained specimens, we tried, but it availed us not."

I thought of Magdalena then, and, in our embrace, how I thought I saw the thinnest purple ephemera in her cheek just below the jawline, and in the delicate blue veins of her throat and wrist. I thought then that it was no more than the magic of our passion, the physical poetry a man induces himself to believe in during the benign madness that holds his thinking during sexual intercourse. Magda, Magda, Magda, I thought. I have become low again. Forgive me please, for I did not know. It did not matter to me that I had appeared only after the Professor had retained Imbroglio to procure Magdalena and the other girl and that I had played no part in the planning of the experiment with the Star Flower. I felt only then that I had assumed a responsibility too late to affect any positive result. I had become the sexton to this venture, the man who leads others into or out of the cemetery at night. The man who buries.

The Phoneutria in the bell jars had all turned to face the pool that held the last of the Star Flowers, and struck their menacing poses with their forelegs in the air, exposing their striped underbellies in a warning, their fangs a chitinous black. The Professor saw this too and rose from his chair carrying his quire of vellum scripts torn from the Pharmacopeia to walk to the edge of the Star Flower's pool. I joined him and we watched the aliens move languidly about the pool. In the silence between us I heard the faintest trace of their cosmic song.

"What life arises from them?" I asked the Professor. "And when will the thing that is to come be brought forth?"

The Professor did not look at me at first, instead maintaining his gaze on his Star Flower's. "There is one more step," he said. "Or so it is written in the index. I need to reread them and check my cipher. I need to make sure."

We walked back to the table and he bade me wait there a moment. He returned with another bottle of the Martell and two snifters. It was not yet noon.

"Thank you for securing the co-operation of Imbroglio in regard to the dead girl," he said. He is a peculiar fellow and I admit, I had some anxiety as to how he might receive that bit of news. I will reimburse you of course, and I insist you take the rest of this Martell back to your room. Think of it as your commission. Tell me, did you know Imbroglio when he, in his other line of work back then, used to go by the unlikely name of Poivre? That's French for 'Pepper.' Mein Gott, he used to call himself Pepper."

The Professor laughed merrily at this memory.

I hardly knew what to say. I thought of the sound Imbroglio's head made when it hit the brick of the fireplace and collapsed into bloody mush. I finally stammered out something of how although I had known of Poivre, I had not chanced to meet him before yesterday, but felt it appropriate that I had at last.

"Let us drink then," said the Professor. "To dwarves and whores."

I seconded and we touched our brandies together and drank the first in one swallow. I needed it. To dwarves and whores indeed.

The brandy seemed to enliven him. He poured us another generous measure and continued to speak. "Have I ever told about how I came to hire the Bashi Bazouk?"

"No," I said, "though I would like to hear it. He seems to be a useful sort, in many ways."

"He's been providential," said the Professor. "I was in Cairo actually, attempting to hire for an expedition to the source of the Blue Nile, looking for such flora yet unnamed as I had heard described there. It is still a dangerous journey you know. The Egyptians, Copts, and Ethiopians I'd hired were a mixed bag at best, and I knew that should things take a turn for the worse out there I might find myself manacled to a Zanzibarian slave trader's pole or possibly merely stripped of purse, watch, and boots, lying face-down on the trail and very, very dead. In short, I needed the kind of right-hand man who could maintain order, when order broke down.

"I made inquiries to certain men who had experience of such things and my inquiry was always the same. 'Where is the baddest man in Cairo whose loyalty can be bought?' I asked them all this same question. Then I'd say, 'If you know such a man, send him to me.' An assortment of cutpurses, cutthroats, and slavers presented themselves. There was even a Pashtun from north of the Kashmir, a fellow very far from home, crop-eared, dead-eyed and in proud possession of an ancient jezail I thought he had to have last fired into Elphinstone's lost army more than fifty years ago. None were suitable. In fact, all were of the exact sort I'd been fearing that I needed to hire guards against.

"Then, on a Friday when the muezzin's call to prayer had emptied the streets – the

Bashi Bazouk came. When he walked through the doorway I thought there'd been an eclipse. He came in alone, without anyone acting as his agent. I asked him to present his letters patent or witnesses, or someone, anyone to speak on his behalf and vouch for his fidelity. He reached into the folds of his sash – the same sash he wears now (at this the Professor pointed at the sleeping man but a few scant feet away from us) and produced two human ears, replete with earrings. I judged these to be taken from some unfortunate women due to the small size of the petrified ears and the earrings, and I note that there had to have been at least two victims because both ears were left ears. The Bashi Bazouks have a violent reputation you know, and not undeserved. Terrified, I hired him on the spot. I was afraid not to. We've been together ever since."

He asked if I'd ever heard the man sing. He sings in Russian, the Professor told me. Songs about love and murder.

"He sings?"

"He does," said the Professor. "Beautifully. Old songs, in an old language."

The Professor got up to relieve himself and left me with my brandy. The Bazouk stirred, then sat up on the couch with his hands on his knees for a time before pressing himself upright. He seemed unsurprised to see me there and by gesture made me get up and follow him. He led me to the dray and there, on the flat bed of it rested my steamer trunk and the canvas that contained the pulp that remained of Imbroglio's man. I understood that he was looking for my assistance for a trip down to the docks.

I walked back into the laboratory to find the Professor humming to himself, already back at his notes with his brandy at hand. I told the Professor that I was off to assist the Bazouk with an errand, and I borrowed a paper and pen to write a note to Magdalena to distract herself however she wanted, I was with the Professor and not back until very late. I sent the note with my hired driver with a generous tip to ensure prompt delivery and with that I dismissed him. I joined the Bazouk then, humming just like the Professor, a lilt only recently learned, composed half of the morning brandy and half of the eerie thrum of the Star Flowers.

VIII: CREMATION

It was only early evening, and with the dray loaded with its stiffening cargo the Bazouk took us by a circuitous path to the docks so as to time our arrival to the best chance of being alone. When we got there, we espied two men hurriedly leaving with a horse and dray not so different from ours, and we saw the expanding ripples in the water as if some heavy cargo had just been let slip within. The Bazouk laughed and I realized the two were no different in their errand than I and the Bazouk. I imagine that the ports of any city are highway above and cemetery below.

We dispatched the dead into the water with the efficiency of men who had done it before, then returned to the cart. The Bazouk drove slowly now, I think he was still tired. His facial expression betrayed no deep thought. I thought him lucky then, to be a man who merely does and does not think any more than he has to.

My own thoughts returned to my conversation with the Professor and our discussion of Chimera. I had omitted what I knew of the Star Flower's effect upon the psyche of its interspecies partner – namely the psychic effect it engendered that produced again within the body and mind the sum total of every sexual experience the partner had ever had, only all at once, and both as a singular experience and a continuum. In light of what the Professor had told me of the Chimera's mandate to harvest the ovum of those it possessed, so that it might, for its own part, continue to make life. I thought this effect both marvelous and sinister. I wondered at the totality of what all might be contained within the organism, and of what, if any, progeny might come. For what did it wait?

Preoccupied thus, I went about the return trip as if in some sort of halting-motion dream like something on Edison's Kinetiscope.

It seemed to me that we arrived at the Professor's home in no time, although it was very dark when we got there.

The Bazouk moved unhurriedly to see to the horse, and I took his leave to enter the laboratory, for the lamps were still lit and I presumed the Professor to still be within. I entered the lab where such a scene greeted me that I can barely describe it, and it seems that each time I remember it, I think of something omitted that I must then add.

I could not see the Professor at first, and called softly to him. It was after all, near to midnight, and it would not do to raise even distant neighbors with some rough shouting. I walked further into the lab and discovered the poor man there, beside one of the surgical tables. He had fallen off the table it seemed, and lay there, obviously dead. His eyes were open, and his mouth fixed in a rictus of a scream, all the signs of a torturous death. He was completely naked, his manhood violently erect. All around his mouth and trailing to the floor was the viscous lilac effluence of the Star Flower, and from where this mucous touched on the floor a seminal trail led back to the shallow pool that he held them in.

I knew at once what he had done.

He'd set the Star Flower on his own face, and, to stimulate the copulatory act, goaded one of the Phoneutria to envenomate him. In our conversation he'd as much prophesied his own death when he'd noted that most men, and all women, die from the venom of the Phoneutria. I cannot imagine the last thirty seconds or so of his life, with the venom of the spider setting every nerve on fire and with the intoxicant of the Star Flower pumping each and every act of his libido through his brain. The spider crawled out from beneath him then, making its way purposefully towards the cover provided by one of the Professor's botanical specimens. I crushed it underneath the heel of my boot without hesitation. Its fangs made an audible crunch.

I looked toward the pool and saw that the Star Flowers within had ceased their slow movements around the water. Nor could I hear their characteristic sub rosa thrumming sound. Their scent, at once both floral and musky, like decay, was overwhelming. I felt in my own head very near to the sensations I'd last had when I'd taken some of that stygian hashish in

Tangiers, while the whore sang her tribal love songs and the kohled young man beside her blundered earnestly into the shock of my wrath.

I understood, then, that the Professor had gleaned from the Pharmacopeia – and from other mysterious books – something I had not: The Star Flower was less a Chimera in its own right than it was the incubator of Chimera. The mere harvest of ova from the women was not enough, it needed a complete zygote to inject itself in to, to make a living thing tripartite. It had harvested the Professor's semen just as it had taken the women's ova, and now all of them, and all of harvests unknown, were now contained within the Star Flower there to be made into something else, a being made not of one or even two, but of many.

Enraged, I moved to the Professor's table and picked up the two remaining bell jars, the furious Phoneutria inside maintaining their combative postures, clicking their black fangs and streaming their clear-running venom against the glass. Each in turn I cast into the Star Flower's pool. Let those soulless murderers drown I thought, and let them take the cursed Chimera with them, if they will.

No sooner had the last Phoneutria gone flailing into the black water than from that same darkness arose the daemon conceived and gestated from the Star Flower's thousand-fold harvest. The head of the creature, five great petals at least as voluminous as the Bazouk's safa, surrounded a maw as black and empty as the void, reached at least to ten feet off of the floor and admitted not a scream, but a roar of such basso profundo rage that it shattered the greenhouse glass. Its body, the same mauve in color as the hematic it filled the two girls and now the Professor with, seemed to be fractals of the head, a thousand – nay, a million – open-mouthed flowers of the same shape and design. Each of these hideous homunculi shouted, shouted, shouted the same insane song, demanding to be released, to be fed, to live.

I thought it my death I was staring at, and I thought I knew something of what Imbroglio must have known when his face was within an inch of the brick of the fireplace in my fine suite of rooms. No sooner had I conceded to the inevitable than I heard another roar, and in rushed the Bazouk holding the same iron bar with which he'd cudgelled Imbroglio's man straight into Hell. He strode to the pool and with one foot on the rim began to swing the bar with all the might and fury his frame possessed.

The bar cut deeply into the daemon and scattered its ichor in gaudy spurts, painting the walls, floor and ceiling in purple gore. At each cut the daemon boomed out its astral rage and the room shook like the timbers were made of straw. Specimens, fertilizers, pots, papers and pens scattered in every direction. Fruits of every sort, some only extant here and but once in the world, due to the Professor's protocols, fell to the floor, splattering and staining, leaving their own seeds half-buried in their pulps.

I thought for a moment that the Bazouk, the most faithful and fearless servant I had ever known, might triumph. But in one movement the thing stepped into him and, ignoring the deepest cuts of the Bazouk's weapon, enveloped him totally. At once it was silent, save for the furious tearing of those open mouths upon open mouths. It lived, it ate, and in short there was nothing organic left of the man who might well have been the last giant to walk this earth.

The daemon boomed again, and the force of its death-song was enough to upset the table that the Professor's notes had once rested on and knock off the lamp. Oil ran from the lamp and ignited, and in seconds the table was aflame along with the thick vellum section of pages the Professor had torn from the Pharmacopeia burned too. The daemon lurched to me on steps so heavy the paving stones beneath it cracked, moving as if to envelope me in the same manner as it had done to render the Bazouk into bloody sustenance for itself.

I snatched up the flaming vellum scripts in one hand and vaulted the table, now turned on its side, and hoped its barrier would afford me some small amount more of life. The conflagration started to rage everywhere that the spilled oil and strewn papers could reach and the daemon moved to within arm's length of me whereupon I reached out to it with the burning pages in my hand and stuffed them into the gut of the creature even as my hand began to char. Many floral mouths shuddered, parted and recoiled at the fire, but not fast enough and the misbegotten thing started to blaze.

Silence fell then, silence from this terrible thing newly born and mortal, and I backed up and hastened to leave the wreck of the laboratory. I saw on the ground, on my side of the overturned table, the whole of the Pharmacopeia still unburnt even after the sacrifice of the excised sheets I'd used to set the daemon on fire. I grabbed them and, now faint with pain from my charred hand, left the building. I collapsed on the small lawn between the lab and the house and looked back into the fire.

The daemon had started to dissolve, each five-petaled fractal detaching itself from the whole and riding the heat and flames into the open sky. They seek a home I thought, these children of Magdalena, Jenny, the Professor, and God only knows what else, these innumerable hosts and astral wanderers aspired to the bosom of some primordial star lost to time and impermanence, and strove, strove with all their will to rise and find their way home, but none soared past the bonds of this earth and the gravity of their flaming host. The licking flames of the monstrosity sucked them back in, searing many into cinders and ending them in ash before they even hit the ground. Those that did collapse and run to ground defeated were soon enough rendered to nothing as well, for only the fire lived and grew.

Arms then, arms and hands pulled at me, urging me to stand and run, lest the fire consume me as well. It was Magdalena, coming from nowhere to rescue me. Unable to raise me by her own strength she knelt to face me and held my face in her hands.

"If you are going to scream," she said, "scream with me. We have but a moment, and it will not last."

I loved her then, for the sound of her voice, and the music of her speech, and it was enough to save me. I raised myself, and with me leaning on her as a crutch, we made our way out to the road and there found our respite from the fire in the darkness of the night.

IX: SINTRA

A fire brigade came, summoned by the neighbors. It bore the same fire mark as did the Professor's house and was crewed by twenty furious and profane Irishmen, brave to the point of recklessness, but such was the fury of the fire that consumed the laboratory they dared not approach it, let alone attempt to quench it, and they were unable to save the house.

"Sometimes we win, and sometimes fire wins," one told me. "There will be others. At least you and your wife are alive."

My seared hand was treated with unguents and balms and gauzes of Egyptian cotton – the remedies of the rich – and today you could not tell that it had ever been burnt. Of the Professor I was told less than one English stone remained of his remains – no more than twenty pounds – and he was buried in a child's casket. Of the Bazouk not enough remained to bury and of the daemon there was not even a trace. Not even the scent remained. Briefly religious, I thanked God for the absence of any sign of the creature.

The Professor's solicitor, an able man named Kruppke, who wore suits of the blackest cloth and was at times confused with the funeral director and pastor both during the process, disposed of the Professor's estate in an orderly fashion. I offered to pay him, but he declined. The Professor was more than solvent he said, and he would be happy to discharge his duty to such a fine man one last time. There was salvaged one bottle of the Martell from the wreck of the house, and Kruppke promptly gifted it to me. Apparently, the Professor had set that much aside for me in writing, with instructions that it be delivered to me wherever I could be found upon the occasion of his passing. He suggested that should all the usual dens of iniquity be found bereft of me, or warrants issued so as to run me to ground far, far away, to try Timbuktu and to look in such opium dens, brandy-parlors, and houses of ill-repute found singly or all in common there. At that I laughed. He knew me well.

I had once remarked that there was nothing he could ask that I would not give. I felt that I had given him nothing. Unprompted, I told Kruppke I had not been as good a friend to the Professor as I should have. I told him that in a way, I thought of the Professor, the Bazouk, and myself as some sort of trinity where the Professor was the head, the Bazouk the heart, and I only the flesh – the weakest part of the trine.

The Professor always had his door open to me, and I had only walked through it on those rare occasions where I felt like it. I would make some sort of gift, expensive but token, and we'd while away a brief time very specifically omitting any talk of my abject failures to do anything with my talent, and my dedication to applying my wealth not to the pursuit of knowledge, but to the enjoyment of vice. That he considered me his apprentice I knew well, and shrugged off, as if it didn't matter. I held to pretensions of collegiality where in fact I should have had the humility to hold myself lucky to be his apprentice. My wealth – inherited wealth – was in no way the equal of his application of science, and I, a fool, persisted in pretending that it was.

I felt I had failed my friend in every way that one can fail a friend, short of actual treachery. If I was less than Absalom in this regard, I was no different in any other.

"You must be an atheist," Kruppke remarked, with a gentle smile.

I admitted to it and asked him how he knew. He told me only that a man of faith confesses to his priest or pastor. An atheist confesses to his solicitor – or in this case, his friend's solicitor – a representative of the mundane. It happens all the time, he said, and is quite alright. After all, the priests and solicitors alike are bound to confidence, and not a word of what I told him would he ever reveal.

He did tell me that for whatever I held it to be worth, he thought that the Professor had deemed me to be the best of friends, and he wanted me to be assured of that. I could see the old man saying that, and this cut me to the quick of my conscience even more so than my belief in the truth of my self-assessment.

I sought to leave the city then, and asked Magdalena if she would come with me, and where she might agree to go. I wanted to offer her a place, not a situation, a place, like she had spoken of to the Bashi Bazouk. A home, I told her, you will have a home if you will it, but you must tell me it is to be so. I can only offer. For a place I suggested San Francisco but she demurred, saying that she might know people there as Dia, and she wanted to go somewhere where no one knew her and she might be introduced as Magdalena or just Magda, just as she was to her parents and friends when she was a girl.

I ended up booking passage to Lisbon, one of the few places I had never been. We made love on the ship every day. We made love for love's sake, and for comfort too. Our passion for each other's flesh had not been so much abated as it had been softened by the experience of the Star Flower and the ruin of the Professor's manor. Often, she would sit atop me and initiate the rhythm of her hips with her hands in my hair, while her own hair, unbound, fell around her shoulders and framed her face in shadows. "Goddess" I would say to her climax, "Goddess, Goddess, Goddess," and our orgasms would come singly, greatly satisfactory if not concurrent with every other one we'd ever had. Done for a time, we would lie together thoughtless but not sleeping, secure in our own company.

I obtained lodgings for us in a grand hotel in the Sintra area north of Lisbon and there we moved among the old nobility and wealthy expatriates of a dozen European nations and the ghosts of their prior generations. We were discreet, solitary for the most part, and belonged to the place with the other quiet habitants in not so very long a time.

She wore the silver denarii at all times and never took it off. She would often hold the coin and thank me, with great sincerity, for her place. I never heard her say anything about at last having a home. I would not bring myself to ask again. I felt that she owed me nothing, not even an answer. I think that for her, the denarii was her place, and I her situation, but that she would forever be reluctant to call anything home. I believed that I had found the limit of what wealth could buy.

One day, when we had gone to the remnants of the chapel of São Pedro de Canaferrim, there among the stones she told me of how she had not had her menses since the events of the Star Flower, and had thought that she was expectant. She confessed that she was by equal turns thrilled and mortified by this, but as time elapsed, she experienced no other symptoms that an expectant mother should have.

At last she had sought out a physician, a London-trained man, who examined her and told her simply that there was nothing wrong with her, no illness or trauma that he could define, and that some women simply ceased to menstruate before others. It is a misfortune for one so young he told her, but not a fatal one, and she might try to content herself with nieces and nephews if she had any, and the children of friends if she had not. He said that if the joys of motherhood were not to be hers than neither were its burdens. The world abounds in children he said, find one or two to spoil then leave them to their parents to raise. It was a very English answer.

She wept there in my arms among the old stones dedicated to São Pedro and I held her in silence. I did not speak of the harvest of the Star Flower nor, of how on the fiery night that ended the creature, how the strange and singing petals that were blown aloft in the fire and incinerated screaming into atoms, were all that ever were of any children she might have had. Such consolation as I had to offer would forever exclude revealing this truth.

The Pharmacopeia, less the pages comprising the index that was immolated with the Professor in the wreck of the laboratory, I sold to a Polish collector named Voynich only a little over a year before the advent of the Great War. Although a professional, and as coy as they come, he seemed greatly pleased to make the purchase for a sum greater than I'd paid for it when I first acquired it for the Professor.

He riffled through the pages once to hear them, and once again to smell them, just as the Professor had on that evening long ago on a continent across the Atlantic.

We shook hands and I told him that I hoped the book would bring him good luck, and he said that he hoped so too. He nodded at Magdalena when he said this, and added that he thought it very likely that the book had already brought me all the good luck it could ever bring one man.

The End

ABOUT THE AUTHOR

Stephen Guy hails from Southern Alberta. He has written many things under a different name, and has been nominated for the Pushcart and Best of the Net Prizes. He once received an honorable mention in a sex-writing contest in the UK, and counts Clark Ashton Smith, The Misfits, and Ernest Dowson among his many influences.

Visit us online at

www.the-seventh-terrace.com

ALSO AVAILABLE

The Seventh Terrace

Terrace VII – Wall of Fire

Trace & Solomon: Torrington

Sleeping Underwater

Tiny Sledgehammer

The Black City Beneath

End of the Loop